TALES FROM CRYPT

VOLUME 5

Introduced by the Old Witch

Story adaptations by Eleanor Fremont

Random House 🏠 New York

The stories in this volume first appeared in different form in *Tales
from the Crypt Comic Books, The Haunt of Fear Comic Books,* and
Shock SuspenStories Comic Books in the following years:

Tales from the Crypt

"Dead Right." Copyright © 1953 by I. C. Publishing Co., Inc.
Copyright renewed 1981 by William M. Gaines, Agent.

"This Wraps It Up." Copyright © 1952 by I. C. Publishing Co., Inc.
Copyright renewed 1980 by William M. Gaines, Agent.

"Bargain in Death." Copyright © 1951 by I. C. Publishing Co., Inc.
Copyright renewed 1979 by William M. Gaines, Agent.

"Last Laugh." Copyright © 1953 by I. C. Publishing Co., Inc.
Copyright renewed 1981 by William M. Gaines, Agent.

The Haunt of Fear

"Minor Error." Copyright © 1952 by Fables Publishing Co., Inc.
Copyright renewed 1980 by William M. Gaines, Agent.

Shock SuspenStories

"In Character." Copyright © 1954 by Tiny Tot Comics, Inc.
Copyright renewed 1982 by William M. Gaines, Agent.

Library of Congress Cataloging-in-Publication Data
Fremont, Eleanor.   Tales from the crypt.
   Adaptation of: Tales from the crypt / William M. Gaines.
   Vol. 1 introduced by the Crypt-Keeper; v. 2 introduced by the Old
Witch; v. 3 introduced by the Vault-Keeper; v. 4 introduced by the Crypt-
Keeper; v. 5 introduced by the Old Witch.
   Vol. 3 adapted by Richard Wenk.
   A collection of horror stories, featuring such grisly characters as a
vampire, werewolf, and murderous madman.
   1. Horror tales, American.   2. Children's stories, American.
3. Horror stories.   4. Short stories.
I. Wenk, Richard. II. Gaines, William M. Tales from the crypt.
PZ7.F8867 Tal   1991   [Fic]   90-23916   ISBN 0-679-81799-9 (v. 1 : pbk.)
ISBN 0-679-81800-6 (v. 2 : pbk.)   ISBN 0-679-81801-4 (v. 3 : pbk.)
ISBN 0-679-83073-1 (v. 4 : pbk.) ISBN 0-679-83074-X (v. 5 : pbk.)

Manufactured in the United States of America   10 9 8 7 6 5 4 3 2 1

CONTENTS

FROM THE
OLD WITCH

 *Greetings and salivations once again, boils and ghouls! Wart's new with you? You'll be pleased to know that the Old Witch has a few surprises up her moldy sleeve for you, you lucky little devils. That's right, another cauldronful of the grossest, creepiest, scariest stories this side of the grave. In fact, some of them are from the other side of the grave. But of course, maybe you weren't expecting disgusting tales. Maybe you thought you were going to get nice stories with talking bunnies. If you did, you'd better leave right now. Quick, before something nasty happens to you. Run! Boo!*

Now, those of you who are left (I knew you'd stay)—where were we? Ah, yes. Disgusting and scary stories. My first literary treat is a cute little tale about a cute little boy. So cute, you could die from it. It's called "Minor Error."

After you've recovered from that one, you'll want to try my next little goody, a tale called "Dead Right." Of course, you're smart enough to know before you even read the story that somebody in it has to be dead wrong. Or maybe just dead. You'll see.

Story number three is called "In Character," and it gives you a gross and gruesome look at what's behind all the glitz and glamour of Hollywood. Or, as we in the Crypt call it, Hollyweird.

Next, we have "This Wraps It Up." It's about three guys who get a bit wrapped up in a problem with a mummy. Not a nice mummy, mind you—more like Mummy Dearest.

Fifthly, we have "Bargain in Death." Some bargain—it turns out to be a bad deal for just about everybody in the story. But that's what happens when you go shopping in graveyards.

Finally, there's "Last Laugh." And that's what Old Witchy is getting, because I'm outta here. I need my beauty sleep, you know. So I'm leaving you all alone with these stories. All alone in the dark. And what was that funny little noise from the basement just now, anyway? Nothing, I'm sure. Heh, heh, heh.

See you next time, my bloodthirsty little buddies. Because, as they say, "You've Got to Have Fiends."

> *Festeringly yours,*
> *The Old Witch*

I hope you're fresh and rested, little fiends, because my first yarn is a <u>draining</u> one. It's about three curious boys. They get into some mischief, of course, but who doesn't? After all, boys will be boys . . . except when they aren't boys at all. Hee, hee.

MINOR ERROR

The old house had stood empty for nearly two years before someone bought it. The kids in the neighborhood had heard that a man and a boy had moved in. But for nearly three months after the moving men had unloaded the furniture, no one had seen the boy.

One summer evening, the neighborhood kids were playing near the front yard of the old house.

"Hey, it's gettin' dark," said Frankie. "Let's play hide-'n-seek."

"Yeah," agreed Butch. "Good idea. How 'bout—"

"Look!" interrupted Pete excitedly. "Looka the old house! There's a face in the window!"

From one of the very top windows the ashen countenance of a twelve-year-old boy peered out at the kids below.

"Gee, that must be the new kid that moved in!" said Butch.

"Gosh, he looks sickly," said Frankie.

"Hey!" called out Pete, cupping his hands to his mouth. "Hey, kid! C'mon out!"

The child's wide-eyed, pale face disappeared from the window.

"He's gone!" said Pete.

"He looked scared stiff," said Frankie.

"Look! The front door!" said Butch.

The front door to the old house opened, and a man came out. He carried a large carton tied with string.

"It's the old guy what bought the house!"

"Gee! Don't he look mean?"

The man did indeed look mean. His face was a rigid mask set with a cruel expression. He started down the street.

"Let's ask him why the kid can't come out an' play!"

"*You* ask 'im. Not me!"

"C'mon, don't be a scaredy-cat. Okay, *I'll* ask. Hey mister!" Pete called out to the man, pretending not to be afraid.

The hard-faced man turned as the kids trotted up to him. "Yeah? What d'yuh want?"

"Say, mister! Why can't your lil' boy come out an' play with us? We ain't even met 'im, and it's been almost three months since you—"

The man's face grew purple with rage. His lips drew back in a snarl, exposing sharp, discolored little teeth. "G'wan! Scram!" His voice was rough and frightening. "Mind your own business! Ezra ain't never coming out! Never, d'you hear? And don't you hang around the house, neither! I don't like pryin'!"

"Gee! S-s-sure, Mister," stammered the frightened boy. "We d-d-didn't mean no harm. We wuz j-j-just askin'."

The man stamped off angrily without saying another word.

"The old crab," muttered Frankie.

"Golly, I'd hate to have *him* as my old man," said Pete.

"I seen him come out every night at this time. Momma says he works at night," said Butch.

The man was halfway down the block now, casting an unpleasant look back at them.

"What's in the box?" whispered Pete.

"I dunno. He never carried it before," said Butch.

"C'mon," said Frankie. "Let's play hide-'n-seek. It's gettin' late." And the three of them sped off to play their game.

The next day, the three kids were all excited about the murder that had happened the previous night. Sitting around Frankie's bedroom, they read the paper avidly.

"It says, 'The murdered man's body was completely drained of its blood.'" read Pete.

"Vampires!" said Butch in an awed voice.

"Aw, shuddup," said Frankie. "There ain't no such thing."

"Oh, no?" retorted Butch. "I read in a comic book once—I think it was called *Tales from the*—"

Pete interrupted, still reading the paper. "Listen to this! 'A carton was found at the scene. It is the police's only clue.'"

"A carton!" said Frankie. "Gee ... last night ..."

"Aw, don't go playin' detective," said Butch.

"Well, he *wuz* carryin' a carton," said Frankie.

"So, what does that mean?" said Pete.

Later that afternoon, the boys were still together.

"What'll we do t'night?" said Butch. "How 'bout playin'—"

Pete stopped him. "How 'bout seein' if we can get to talk to that new kid?"

"Not me, boy," said Frankie. "His old man was awful mean."

"Aw, c'mon," said Pete. "The sourpuss works at night. We'll wait until he leaves."

And so, toward evening, the three boys

waited behind a tree and watched the house until they saw the man leave.

"There he goes!" said Frankie under his breath. "He's got a carton again!"

"We'll wait till he turns the corner," Butch whispered.

"Poor kid," said Pete, glancing up at the high window. "He never gets out."

Finally, the man disappeared around the corner. The kids hurried across the street, shouting:

"Hey, kid!"

"Hey, Ezra!"

"C'mon out!"

The door to the old house creaked open, and a pale white face appeared. It was Ezra. He had jet-black hair and huge eyes, and he was wearing a bow tie. Poor kid. He even had to dress funny.

"Hi, Ezra," said Frankie, a little shyly.

"Hi, Ez," said Pete.

Ezra looked like a startled deer. "G...Go away!" he said. "If my uncle . . ."

"Yer uncle?" said the flabbergasted Pete. "Golly! It ain't his old man!"

"If my uncle finds out I spoke to you," Ezra

went on, "he'll . . . he'll . . ." He looked at the floor.

"Why don't yer uncle let you come out an' play, Ez?" asked Butch.

"I don't know," said Ezra forlornly. "He doesn't want me to talk to anybody."

"Where's yer mom 'n pop?" asked Pete. "Huh? Why do you live with *him?*"

Ezra jammed his hands into his pockets and kept looking at the floor. "M-m-my mother and father are d-d-dead. Uncle takes c-c-care of me n-n-now."

"Gee, that's too bad," said Frankie.

"Hey, Ez," said Pete, "yer shivering. Better put somethin' on."

"Y-y-yes. I'll be right back."

Ezra went into the house. He came out again with a jacket draped around his shoulders—a jacket that was much too long for him.

"It—it's one of my uncle's suit coats," he explained. "I don't have many clothes."

Butch's jaw dropped. "Hey!" he yelled. "Look! On the jacket!"

"Bloodstains!" said Pete.

Ezra looked down at the coat. "Huh?" he said. "Oh. Uncle is always getting stains on his jackets. *I* have to wash them out."

"Stains like *them?* Bloodstains?" said Pete.

"Uh-huh," said Ezra dully.

"W-w-well, s-s-s'long, Ezra," stammered Pete, backing away. "We'll see yuh again."

"Yeah! G'bye, Ezra. See yuh." Frankie was halfway off the porch already.

The kids thundered down the block as though something were chasing them.

"I *told* yuh the old crab did it!" wheezed Butch as they raced away.

"He's a vampire, all right!" Frankie agreed.

"Gee! Golly!" was all Pete could say.

The next day, the kids read about the second strange killing. Pete held the newspaper up and read from it once again.

"Jus' like the first one!" he said. "Blood drained an' all!"

"An' they found another empty carton," said Frankie, reading over Pete's shoulder.

"What'll we do?" said Butch, pacing the room. "If we tell the cops Ezra's uncle is a vampire . . ."

"We're not sure yet," said Frankie. "We've got to be sure."

That night, the kids crouched behind the bushes opposite Ezra's house and waited for the man to come out.

"Here he comes," said Pete. "He's carryin' a carton again!"

"Shh," warned Frankie. "We'll follow him . . . but stay out of sight."

Ducking behind fences, lampposts, and trees, the kids followed Ezra's uncle. He walked all the way across town, finally slowing down near the side of an abandoned warehouse.

"He's stopping!" said Frankie.

"Someone's comin' the other way!" Butch observed.

The boys watched the shadows play on the warehouse wall, in the light of the street lamp. They saw a second man walking ... the shadow of Ezra's uncle, with its peaked cap, following behind ... Ezra's uncle raising his arm high above the head of the other man ... something large, like a baseball bat, in his hand coming down ...

"He's hittin' him on the head!" hissed Butch.

"I'm gettin' out of here!" Pete whispered.

"Shh," cautioned Frankie.

"He's takin' somethin' out of the carton!" said Butch.

They moved a little closer so they could get a better view.

"It . . . it's a gallon jug!" said Frankie.

"Holy cow! He's drainin' the blood into the jug!" Pete clapped both hands over his mouth to keep from retching.

"I feel sick," moaned Butch.

"C'mon," said Frankie. "We've seen enough."

The three of them couldn't get out of there soon enough. They walked home on rubbery legs beneath a full moon.

"No wonder he keeps Ezra locked up!" said Butch. "He's afraid Ezra'll talk!"

"We gotta do somethin'!" said Pete.

"The cops'll never believe Ezra's uncle is a vampire," said Frankie.

"Then we've got to destroy him ourselves," said Butch resolutely. "Vampires sleep during the day. Now, here's what we'll do. . . ."

Their whispers followed them all the way down the street as they headed home.

The next day, the kids climbed through a window of Ezra's house, armed with a hammer and a sharpened wood stake. They crept through the hallways, looking into the musty rooms.

"There he is! Asleep, just like I said," said Butch, pointing into the room at the end of the hallway.

Ezra's uncle was lying in a great bed, his face twisted into an ugly scowl even in sleep. He was snoring lightly.

"Put the stake over his chest!" Pete urged. "Hurry, before he wakes up!"

Frankie got the stake into position, and Pete raised the hammer as high as he could.

"Okay! Slam it hard!" said Butch.

"Quick!" said Frankie, squeezing his eyes shut.

"Here goes," said Pete, bringing the hammer down.

Shrieks of pain echoed through the house as the hammer fell upon the stake again and again. Finally, it was over.

"He . . . he's . . . dead," gasped Pete.

"He . . . he's supposed to fall into dust!" said Butch, looking at the dead man.

"Aw, you an' your comic books," said Frankie.

Pete looked around. "C'mon," he said. "Let's go find Ezra."

The kids searched the house, upstairs and down, but there was no sign of Ezra. Suddenly, Pete and Frankie heard a shout from Butch. He was down in the basement.

"Hey! Down here!" he yelled. "In the cellar! Oh . . . *golly!*"

"C'mon!" said Frankie. He and Pete ran down the stairs to the cellar.

Butch stood before the open coffin, staring with wide, frightened eyes. Ezra slept serenely.

His bloodstained lips were curled in a slight smile. The empty gallon jug stood on the floor behind his coffin.

"H-he . . . he's asleep!" said Frankie.

In an instant, the full truth of the situation swept over all three of them.

"*H-He's* the vampire!" cried Pete.

"We . . . we made a mistake!" said Butch. "A *big* mistake!"

You sure did make a mistake, Butch, my boy. But that's because you didn't read my stories very carefully. Vampires sleep in coffins, not beds. And they drink blood—they don't collect it. Yep, good ol' Ezra was the vampire. So were his mommy and his daddy. Uncle was just taking care of him because he loved the child. Of course, that meant getting blood for the thirsty lil' tyke. At least till he was old enough to go out and get his own. Bet you wish somebody loved you that much, huh?

The next story, my slimy little darlings, is about a friendship that came to a grave end. Let this be a lesson to you. If you think it's a bad idea to have any friends at all, you're . . .

DEAD RIGHT

Joseph Fairbanks and I had been lifelong friends. We'd met in medical school, and our friendship had grown through our internship and on into our practicing years. Joseph had become one of the nation's outstanding surgeons, and I'd enjoyed no small success as a heart specialist.

Neither of us had married, and consequently, as we'd grown older, we'd sought each other's company more and more to fill the loneliness of bachelor life. Since neither Joseph nor I had a family, we had arranged our wills so that we were each other's inheritors.

When our virile days had passed, and a contentment with just sitting by an open fire and sipping brandy had come upon us, we'd made it a point to visit each other's homes at least once a week, usually on Friday nights.

I would enter his foyer, handing my hat and cane to his manservant.

"Good evening, Joseph!" I would say to my old friend.

"Come in, Carl! Come in!" he would say heartily.

Each Friday when the weather was cold, we would settle ourselves into the comfortable wing chairs before his roaring fire, and I would hold my hands out to warm them.

"Will it be the usual? Brandy?" Joseph would always ask me.

"Yes, Joseph," I'd reply. "Ahhh . . . the fire feels good tonight. This damp weather always settles in my bones."

Of course, Joseph and I had had our differences, too—like that silly theory of his that he would unfailingly bring up every time we were together. We would not be conversing for ten minutes before it would come up once again. A typical argument would go this way:

"But actually, Carl," he'd say, "how do we *know?* How do we know a man is really dead? Who's to say that he cannot hear or see or feel what is going on around him?"

"Because, my dear Joseph," I would counter, "his heart has stopped. The blood no longer flows to his brain. The cells die for lack of oxygen!"

I think that the older we'd gotten, the more childish we'd become about this continuous disagreement over Joseph's ridiculous theory. We'd come to fight over it as two children fight over who's to be "it" in tag.

"But isn't it possible, Carl," Joseph would argue, "that the sensory functions of the body can continue after what we presumptuously call 'death'?"

"If the brain cells die," I'd say, "sensory functions cease."

"Ah . . . that is the point, Carl. Suppose the brain cells do not die minutes after the heart stops. Suppose they continue to live for hours . . . maybe days?"

"But we know that brain cells cannot last fifteen minutes without oxygen!"

"In their normal state, yes. But suppose that at the moment of heart cessation—whether through bodily injury or simple heart failure— suppose that the brain cells go into a state of shock, of reduced metabolism."

"Reduced metabolism? Shock?" I would scoff. "How ridiculous!"

"Ridiculous? No! Possible! Very possible! In a state of shock, in which the functions of the brain cells have been curtailed, the little oxygen left in the protoplasm at the moment of heart failure would be enough to prolong the life of the cells for hours," Joseph would insist.

"So a dead man is not really dead when he is pronounced dead, eh? He can still feel and see and hear, although he cannot move . . . ?" I'd shake my head.

"Exactly! Think of the number of corpses

you've seen whose eyes are still open . . . whose eyes we thoughtfully press closed with pennies or wads of cotton. Think of the horror of having your eyes forced shut and held shut . . . when your eyes can still see."

"Joseph! This theory of yours is sheer poppycock!"

But he would keep talking, undeterred by my opposition. "Think of the horror of listening to your blood being pumped from your body . . . of embalming fluid being forced in. The pain! The excruciating pain! And listening to your own funeral ceremony . . . feeling the closeness of the coffin . . . the lid slamming down . . . perhaps being nailed shut!"

"Stop it, Joseph!" I would shout.

"Think of feeling yourself being lowered into the grave . . . the thumping of earth being shoveled down on top of you . . . and then— only then—fading and actually dying!"

"Good lord, Joseph! I shall leave this minute if you persist in continuing this ghoulish conversation!"

As I have said, we were just like children. I always had to threaten to leave in order to get Joseph to stop his nonsense. The rest of the evening would be pleasant, and we'd remain the best of friends.

But last night was different. Last night was very different.

As usual, I had walked into Joseph's home and handed my hat and cane to his manservant. As usual, the comfortable chairs were arranged before the fire.

"Sit down, Carl," said Joseph. "Will it be the usual? Brandy?"

"Yes, Joseph, brandy will be fine."

Last night, we sat in front of the fire, sipping our brandies, and Joseph didn't once bring up his ridiculous theory. Instead, he talked of investments and bad luck and some such nonsense. I didn't pay much attention. The fact is, I'd thought of a new argument against his theory, and I was waiting, mulling it over in my mind.

"So you see, Carl," I heard him say, "I'm bankrupt."

Suddenly, I was startled into paying attention. "Eh? Wha—Joseph! Did you say you're *bankrupt?*"

"That's right, Carl. And I'm badly in debt. I need money. A great deal of money."

"Why, I'll gladly lend you what you need, Joseph," I offered.

"Lend, Carl?" he said, looking me straight in the eye. "Lend? Don't be silly! I'm taking it! Your whole fortune! You see, I've poisoned your brandy!"

"*Joseph!*" I cried. "*No!*"

I staggered to my feet. I felt weak and dizzy, and my legs and arms were tingling.

"Don't bother trying any emetics to make you vomit the stuff up, Carl," he said, cackling with pleasure. "The poison is a fast-acting one. You'll be dead in a moment."

"Joseph!" I said, slurring my words badly now. "How could you . . . ?"

I was halfway across the room when I simply collapsed to the floor. I tried to move. I tried to speak. It was as though I were completely paralyzed.

"Good-bye, Carl," said Joseph cheerfully. "Thank you for the inheritance."

He came and stood over me. I could see clearly, yet I couldn't move my eyes. They were glued in one position. Joseph moved into my line of vision and knelt beside me. I felt him lift my limp hand.

"No pulse," he said with satisfaction. "You're dead, Carl. Stone dead."

Dead? How could I be dead? I could *see* . . . I could *feel* . . . I could *hear* Joseph dialing the telephone.

"Hello, Norton Funeral Parlor? That you, Ben? This is Doctor Joseph Fairbanks. You'd better get over here and bring your big wicker basket. Doctor Carl Winston has just died. Yes, at my house. Heart attack."

I lay paralyzed on the floor, sending desperate thoughts across the room: "No! Oh, please! *No!*"

I heard Joseph hang up. I heard him approach, and I saw his face when he leaned over me—his leering face.

"Poor Carl," he said. "How we used to argue about silly theories ... theories that I didn't believe myself!"

Oh, lord, what he was saying to me ... thinking I couldn't hear ... knowing I was dead.

"But I never could get you angry enough, could I, Carl?" he went on. "I never could get you so upset you'd drop dead! No! I had to poison you to get your money ... your estate!"

Then, a pain ... a horrible, excruciating pain in my chest ... and Joseph grinning down at me and bragging.

"It will be simple, Carl. I'm a physician. I'll sign the death certificate. Death by natural causes. No one will question a surgeon's word. Ah ... the bell. The undertaker is here."

Ben Norton came in looking very sad. As soon as Ben was in the room, Joseph's tone changed. Now, as he spoke, he sounded genuinely bereaved.

"It was awful, Ben!" he said, a catch in his voice. "Awful! One minute, sitting and drinking. The next minute, dead!"

"How'd it happen, Doc?" Ben asked solemnly.

"We were arguing about something or other. A medical theory of mine. Carl was shouting. He must have become too emotionally upset. His heart . . ."

"Too bad," said Ben. "Such a nice guy. Well . . . I'll get his body downtown."

"I'll go with you, Ben," said Joseph. "Oh . . . since I'm the only one in the world Carl had—no family, you know—there's no use dragging this out. Arrange for a small, dignified funeral tomorrow. . . ."

"Sure," said Ben. "Why waste time? I got my wicker basket in the trunk. C'mon and help me."

You . . . you who are reading this story! How can you understand how I felt? How can you know the horror that crept up my rigid spine? I was dead . . . dead by all the standards. And yet I could *feel* . . . could *hear* . . . could *see* things move as they lifted me and placed me into the basket.

"Yep, nice guy," said Ben as they were lifting me into the wicker. "The doc was a nice guy."

"Heavy, though," said Joseph. "Heavy people are more apt to suffer heart trouble."

I could see them looking down at me. But I couldn't blink . . . couldn't move an eyelid . . . couldn't live—ever again.

Joseph's face was very near mine. "Look, Ben," he said, staring into my face. "His eyes . . ."

"Yeah, I know," said Ben. "They're open, almost like he was seein' us, eh? Well . . ."

Ben reached down and I felt his fingertips touch my eyelids, pushing them closed. And

now I was shrouded in the darkness of death. But I could still hear. I could still feel them lift the basket and carry me. I could imagine what was happening. They were putting me into the back of the black panel truck with the black-curtained windows.

"Easy, now," said Joseph as they slid me in.

"Why?" said Ben. "He can't feel the bumps."

I could hear them get in the front . . . hear the engine start . . . feel the motion of riding, riding into town to the funeral parlor . . .

"Well," said Joseph at last, "here we are."

"Help me get him out," said Ben.

I could hear the back doors open again. I could feel the basket being lifted and carried into the cold white room with the needles and tubes. I could smell the perfume that tried to hide the formaldehyde odor.

"Put it down here," said Ben.

I could feel myself being lifted . . . being placed on a cold surface . . . a marble table . . .

"I'll get things ready. Care to watch?" Ben offered.

"I don't mind," said Joseph.

I could hear the rustling whisper of hoses,

the sharp clinking of bottles, the hum of pump motors starting . . .

"First, we drain the blood," said Ben matter-of-factly.

"I see," said Joseph.

I felt what must have been a needle entering my arm. But there was no pain. Joseph had been wrong. There was no pain, even as the last drop of blood dripped out of my body and I heard it gurgling down a drain somewhere. . . .

"Now the embalming fluid," said Ben.

"Oh," said Joseph.

Another pump. Another needle pressing

against my dead flesh. More gurgling.

"I'll see about a coffin," said Ben.

"Not too expensive, now," said Joseph.

Joseph didn't want to see his money wasted. *Not too expensive.* I wanted to scream. But how could I? Dead men don't scream. They only lie stiffly . . . listening . . . feeling . . . and crying inside. . . .

"This one will do," said Ben. "Reasonable, too. Help me get him into it."

"Fine," said Joseph.

I was being lifted again. Now I could feel the smooth satin against my dead hands. The camphor smell of newness. I was being put into my coffin.

"There," said Ben.

"Now," said Joseph, "you'll arrange everything? The funeral plot?"

How long I lay there I do not know. Perhaps time, to one dead, is immeasurable. The lid was slamming down. . . .

"Let's go," said Joseph.

The lid was being nailed. . . .

"The chapel is filled," said Ben. "They're waiting."

I was being moved again. A voice, eulogizing me. My funeral oration . . . I was hearing it all.

"And so," said the preacher's voice, "in parting, may I add . . . Carl Winston lived, and he died. But his memory—his work—lives after him."

A motor. The coolness of open air. I was being lowered into the grave. The voice: "Ashes to ashes . . . dust to dust . . ."

The hollow boom of dirt crashing down upon the coffin lid. The horror . . . the screaming, silent horror of it . . .

And now the shoveling has stopped. There is laughter and voices.

"That's enough," I hear Ben's voice say.

"All right, open it up," says Joseph.

The lid is creaking open. A rush of fresh air caresses my face.

Joseph is leaning over me, speaking loudly. "Carl! Are you convinced? *Are you?*"

"Open his eyes," said Ben.

A finger touches my eyes. The night stars twinkle down at me. Joseph's face cuts across them, blocking them out.

"You're paralyzed, Carl," he said. "You're not really dead! It's a new kind of anesthetic! I put it into your brandy!"

Joseph grins at me. Ben Norton is beside him.

"We *staged* this, Carl . . . Ben and I, together! You're in the garden out in back of my house."

"It isn't morning yet, Carl," said Ben.

Joseph leaned closer to my face. "The drug will be wearing off soon," he said to me.

"We didn't even go to the funeral parlor!" said Ben. "I just drove you around."

"Then we brought you back to the house, into my office. We pretended it was the funeral parlor," Joseph told me.

Ben grinned. "I lent Doc Fairbanks a few of my pumps for sound effects—and this coffin."

"It was a *gag,* Carl. I wanted to show you that my theory could be right! You almost believed it, didn't you, Carl? *Didn't you?*"

Ben looked at his watch. "Doc," he said anxiously. "It's five-thirty. Shouldn't he be coming out of it?"

It's morning now. The stars have gone, and I feel the sun on my face. Joseph is pleading with me, tears in his eyes. Ben Norton's face just gets paler and paler.

"Carl!" shouts Joseph, his face drenched in sweat. "For God's sake, Carl! Come out of it! It's a gag, Carl! Come out of it! Please!"

Ben just stared straight ahead of him. "Oh, lord help us," he said softly.

Poor Joseph and his theory. He wanted so much for me to accept it. And now I *have* accepted it! Only, he won't know he's right. Not until he goes through what I've gone through. For I *am* dead. I died of a heart attack, just before the undertaker came.

Heh, heh! So next time you meet a corpse, my wee ones, be careful what you say, eh? You might hurt its non-feelings. Well, I think it's time for us to move on to my next little morsel. Ahem. Koff, koff. Hack, hack. I seem to be having a coffin fit. It must have been that gag. Get it? Gag? Koff, koff.

 *We now go, my little cabbages, to the hallowed hills of Hollywood, the land of true horror: smog, freeway traffic, <u>reruns</u>, for heaven's sake. But in case you need more evidence, take a look at this gruesome little tale of terror from the other side of the cameras. . . .*

IN CHARACTER

A sudden hush fell over the lavishly decorated executive dining room of Magnus Pictures, Inc., and for the moment the musical ring of silver on expensive china and the loud, bragging prattle of pompous, overweight movie executives came to a halt. A testimonial dinner was in progress. Having called for silence, Lawrence B. Maynor, president of Magnus Pictures, stood smiling down at the mild-mannered, aging man seated to his right. Maynor held up a simple gold watch. There was a scattering of halfhearted applause. Then he began to read the message engraved on the back of the watch, a message to the guest of honor:

"'To Bela Kardiff, in memory of a fabulous

39

era, from the executive staff of Magnus Pictures, Inc., June 4, 1954.'"

Bela Kardiff rose slowly to accept the token of appreciation, his sad eyes dimmed with tears. He took the glittering watch in his hands and read the inscription. Then he looked at the men seated around the small horseshoe-shaped table. His voice was barely audible as he began to speak.

"I . . . I want to thank you all for honoring me here tonight . . . for this dinner . . . this watch . . . for my whole career," he said softly.

He placed the watch on the table and hesitated, as if contemplating his next words. Then he picked up the large bottle of champagne before him.

"I would like to propose a toast . . . a toast that says thank you for all that you have done for me."

The champagne cork popped loudly as Bela pulled it from the bottle neck. He turned and began to walk behind the men seated at the table.

"Perhaps chronological order would be the best way to make this toast," he said quietly.

"So I'll start with the first of you that I ever knew."

Bela stopped behind the seat of a portly mustached man, and slowly poured him a glass of champagne.

"To Don Muller, my agent," he said as he poured, "who discovered me and first started me down the road to fortune and success."

Don Muller smiled self-consciously as Bela Kardiff looked down at him.

"Remember, Don?" Bela asked. "Remember the lean days before I became a star? Remember how I used to come to your office each day . . . begging . . . *begging* for work? And you would shake your head.

"Nobody wanted an English-professor type, you told me, Don. They were looking for gangster types, or dashing hero types, you said. Muscle men.

"I begged you for a cab driver role, Don," Bela continued. "An elevator operator . . . a waiter . . . anything! I was flat broke.

"Remember the morning that call from Magnus came in, how you listened and nodded and looked at me all the while?" said Bela, bending over his tuxedoed agent. "They wanted someone tall, someone unknown. A makeup part.

"Remember how you hung up, Don, and turned to me?" said Bela, smiling. "'Look, Bela, I got a part for you!' you said. 'It's a big part! Good money! A chance! It's not what you'd want, but it could be a beginning!'

"'What? What is it?!' I said that morning. I was desperate!

"Magnus Pictures was taking a flyer on a new gimmick, you told me. Horror movies!

They were going to do a Hollywood version of *Frankenstein*. They were looking for somebody to play the monster."

Bela Kardiff was pacing back and forth behind Don Muller's chair now, telling the story like the actor he was.

"I didn't think I wanted to take a monster part. I didn't think that was the kind of work I was cut out for. It just didn't feel right. I hesitated.

"Remember how you delivered your ultimatum, Don?" said Bela. "'Look, Bela,' you said to me. 'You owe me a nice hunk of dough. Either you take this part, or I drop you cold!'"

Bela turned away from Don Muller, and returned to the speaker's chair—to Lawrence B. Maynor, president of Magnus Pictures. He filled Maynor's champagne glass slowly.

"Remember that, Larry?" he said to Maynor. "You were just a casting director then. You were only partway up the ladder to the top."

Maynor beamed, thinking about how far he'd come.

"Remember how I came to you?" asked Bela. "It was on the soundstage of *Franken-*

stein. You were rushing around with your clipboard, and I had a little trouble getting your attention.

"I told you that Don Muller had sent me over, that I'd come to audition for the monster role. I asked you what I should read.

"'Read?' you said with a guffaw. 'There's nothing to read. This is a Hollywood version of the Shelley book. The monster doesn't talk in our version!'

"I was crushed, Larry," said Bela. "I protested. I was an actor! If there were no lines at all, what kind of a part was it for me?

"'Listen, whatever your name is,' you said, Larry. 'Magnus Pictures is on the rocks. One more flop, and we're bankrupt. So we're gonna produce a moneymaker, a horror picture to end all horror pictures. If you want the part, okay. If not, I'll get somebody else.' And you turned away."

Bela moved down the table, and poured another glass of champagne.

"So I took the part," he said as he poured. "My stomach screamed louder than my pride. And that's when I met you, George Robins. It was you who dreamed up the publicity scheme.

" 'We'll play up the monster,' you said, George. 'We'll bill him as the star . . . this Kardiff guy! We'll tell the public he's the most horrible thing that ever walked across a movie screen.' "

There was a tiny smile on Bela Kardiff's face as he remembered George Robins with his plaid suit and bald head, pacing up and down the room, waving his arms in excitement.

"You had an ambulance parked outside the theater on preview night, George! You had people scared before they even went in!"

Don Muller, Lawrence Maynor, and George Robins chuckled at this little trip down memory lane.

Bela moved on, stopping at the chair of Sidney Chase, treasurer of Magnus Pictures. Chase was a large, florid gentleman.

"*Frankenstein* was a big hit," said Bela as he poured Chase's champagne. "It made three times its initial investment, didn't it? And the public clamored for more. They clamored for more of this frightening, horrible star you'd discovered.

"I was there in your office, Sidney, when you had a conversation with Larry," said Bela.

"You called me a gold mine. You said, 'We've got to make more horror pictures with Kardiff! How about *Dracula?*'

"First, a man-made monster," said Bela in his soft, cultured voice. "Next, a vampire. After *Dracula* opened, my name became synonymous with horror and mayhem and death. Me . . . Bela Kardiff. Harmless, quiet, mild-mannered Bela Kardiff." He stopped pouring champagne.

"I remember the first time it happened, the first incident on the street. It was a mother and her little boy. When he saw me, he clung to her in terror. 'Look, Mama!' he cried. 'It's *him!*' And he screamed. The mother held her child tightly, and looked at me with such hatred. 'You . . . you ought to be ashamed of yourself,' she said bitterly. 'Going around frightening children!'

"I tried to stop the mad avalanche that was burying me. Remember, Milton?"

He stopped before the chair of the next man, and poured him a glass of champagne.

"Remember when I came to see you, Milton?" asked Bela. "I begged you to give me a chance at a decent dramatic part. I didn't want to be typecast anymore!

"'Look, Bela,' you said. 'I'm only a producer. I do what the boys upstairs tell me. Your next picture is *The Mummy's Hand*.'"

Bela sighed. "I was a mummy . . . a werewolf . . . a zombie . . . everything sinister and despicable and ugly. I murdered again and again on the screen. Over and over I sat in screening rooms, looking at movies that revolted me, while you raved.

"And so, while each of you moved up the

executive ladder, I sank lower and lower." He turned to Larry Maynor. "Remember when I came to see you, to plead with you, Larry?" said Bela. "You were president by then. All you had to do was say the word. I begged you to give me a chance at something else!

"You looked at me and smiled. 'I'd be crazy, Bela,' you said cheerfully. 'You're worth a fortune as you are! Why kill the goose that lays the proverbial golden egg?'

"Oh, I don't deny that I was financially rewarded for this degradation. I had a nice home in Beverly Hills, a swimming pool, a chauffeured car, everything a star should have ... except my pride.

"Remember when you came into my house waving a manuscript, Don?" said Bela, turning to his agent. "'Got the new script, Bela,' you said. 'You play a ghoul in this one.'

"'Not a ghoul!' I said. 'That's too much!'

"But I played the part. I hated to, but I was trapped by then. At the preview of *The Hideous Ghoul* I mingled with the crowd in the theater lobby and heard what they were saying:

"'Same old thing.'

"'Definitely a B-picture.'

" 'Magnus better start trying other things!'

"It was the beginning of the end. The public was tired of horror pictures. *The Hideous Ghoul* lost money. The next—*Frankenstein Meets a Werewolf*—in which I played both parts, was a miserable failure.

"Remember, Sid? Remember what you said to me then? You were dropping horror pictures. They were no longer a moneymaking proposition.

"That was fine with me. I was happy to be done with them. I was eager to see what plans Larry had for me.

"So I came to see you, Larry.

" 'Sorry, Bela,' you said to me. 'You're typed. We couldn't use you for anything genteel. The public will always associate you with horror and death.'

"I leaned across your desk. Remember, Larry? 'You mean I'm through, Larry,' I said. 'Washed up . . . finished! That's what you mean!'

"And then I went to you, Milt. I pleaded for a chance. I could act—I just needed one chance!

"You looked at me so coolly, Milt, 'I'd be

49

out of my mind, Bela,' you said. 'If horror comes back, I'll give you a ring.' "

Bela stood beside the table, staring straight ahead, remembering.

"I was a has-been . . . a faded star. I had to sell my place in Beverly Hills. I was broke.

"I slipped down . . . down. I left Hollywood for New York. I tried radio. Read my lines as well as I could: 'Good evening, mystery fans. This is your host in chills, Bela Kardiff, welcoming you once more to the terror theater. . . .'

"But the sponsor was unimpressed. 'It was good once,' he said. 'But this stuff is old hat now. We'll have to cancel.' So that was it for my career in radio.

"A second-rate Broadway producer managed to gather enough financial backing using my name to star me in a horror play. There I was again, in my monster getup, saying to a cringing victim, 'Yes, Smiley . . . I've come back. . . .' What garbage!

"The critics panned it, of course. The play closed. The backers lost a fortune, and I never got my salary. The producer skipped. I was forced to borrow.

"I bumped into you now and then, George. Do you remember? I borrowed money from you. Not much. But it was too much for you.

"'This is my last handout, Bela,' you said when I came back to you, desperate. 'I've got my own troubles.'

"I managed to scrape along. I slept in cheap hotels. The desk clerks thought I was the funniest thing in the world. 'Well, if it isn't the spook man himself,' they'd say. 'Who'd you

murder today, "Frankenstein"?'

"I ate in dives. Just trying to get a cup of coffee was an ordeal. 'Well, look who's haunting my joint!' the owners would joke in their heavy-handed way. 'Dracula! In person!'

"It was TV that saved me from ending up on skid row. TV was in its infancy then, and it was hungry for names—even has-been names.

"I did an awful show, and it paid terribly. The producer apologized to me as he handed me $350. But I was happy to have the work.

"Of course, it was a horror show. What else could it be? But it fed me for two months. And then I got another call . . . and another. I wasn't getting rich, but at least I was working. They stuck cameras in my face and made me grimace. I didn't care."

Bela Kardiff finished pouring the last glass of champagne for the last guest. "They tell me it was your idea, Eddie," he said. "This testimonial dinner. Eddie Backman, my old cameraman."

Eddie blushed modestly. "Well, Bela, I . . ."

"You certainly did your job well, Eddie," said Bela. "Back in those days, *you* put me on film in all my horror . . . all my vileness and evil."

"It was my job, Bela," said Eddie.

Bela turned and strode back to his seat. He picked up his glass and looked into it pensively. "Of course, Eddie," he said. "I understand. You *had* to make me horrible. You, too, George. And you, Milt . . . Sid . . . Don . . . Larry. You all had to."

Bela lifted his glass high. "You all did what you had to do. And so, I offer this toast . . . to the things you all did for me!"

The men around the table stood nervously and drained their glasses.

And Bela Kardiff smiled.

"You know, gentlemen," he said, "wherever I went after my star faded here in Hollywood, I could never escape those things you did for me. I could never live down the stereotype you'd cast of me . . . the horror character . . . the murderer. So I finally accepted it!"

He put down his untouched glass of champagne.

"I am what you made me, gentlemen. I put strychnine in your champagne!"

He took a certain grim pleasure in watching them shriek, clutch their throats, begin choking, and fall to the floor.

All right, all right, so you saw the end coming a mile away. But the question is, why didn't all those guys who got poisoned? How come they weren't smart enough to figure out Bela's little game? <u>Because they're the people who invent sitcoms, that's why!</u>

 *Hey, kiddies, I bet you didn't know I've joined a wrap group. It's called King Tut and the Undead. We're all very well preserved for our age. When you get up into the high two thousands, those little wrinkles can really show. Well, I gotta go now. My mummy's calling me.*

THIS WRAPS IT UP

The flaming Egyptian sun blazed down upon the three archaeologists, sending sweat down their faces in tiny streams. They worked feverishly—first one, then the other—digging into the burning sand at the base of the towering cliff.

"It's got to be here!" exclaimed one of the men. "It's got to! Every shred of evidence we've pieced together says this is the spot!"

"Don't be disappointed if it isn't, Arnold. We've been wrong before," cautioned one of the others. "Why don't you rest now? Remember—your heart . . ."

Doctor Arnold Munsen sat down and

wiped his soaking face with his handkerchief. He studied his two associates, Professor Thomas Steel and Doctor Jerome Grabel, as they continued digging.

"Here we are," said Arnold, "on the verge of the most valuable archaeological find of the century, and I have to watch my heart!"

"You were advised against coming on this expedition, Arnold," said Jerome. "You shouldn't even be touching a shovel."

"Bah," said Arnold. "I'm as healthy as a twenty-year-old. Just because I had a slight heart attack—"

"Another heart attack could be fatal, Arnold!" said Thomas. "Get that through your stubborn skull!"

"Tom! Arnold! Look!" gasped Jerome. He was pointing at the spot where they'd been digging.

"What is it, Jerome?" Thomas's voice was tense.

"You've found something!" said Arnold.

"The entrance! The entrance to the tomb!" exclaimed Jerome.

At the bottom of the excavation was a round iron ring imbedded in a huge, partially uncovered slab of stone.

Arnold elbowed his way to the front of the group. "Give me a shovel!" he said. "Let me—"

Thomas restrained him. "Arnold! Take it easy! Please!"

"I'll finish uncovering the slab," said Jerome.

Soon the stone block had been fully cleared of sand. As Arnold watched anxiously, Thomas and Jerome tugged at it.

"It's coming loose!" said Arnold. "I'll give you a hand."

"We . . . can . . . manage, Arnold," grunted Thomas.

"A little more," panted Jerome, wrenching the huge stone a quarter of an inch farther.

Finally the large slab was shifted far enough to reveal a dark opening with dusty steps that descended into the blackness. The musty odor of decay and rot, of things long buried and air three thousand years old, seared their nostrils. But they didn't mind at all.

"We've found it! We've found it!" shouted Jerome. The three grown men danced around like children.

"The tomb of Ikah-Mu-Kahma, fifth pharaoh of Egypt!" crowed Arnold.

As they made their way downward, their footsteps echoed into the cavernous blackness, shattering the silence of centuries. Flickering light from the lantern Thomas carried caressed walls that had not seen light for over a hundred generations. The three men descended into the shaft.

"I've counted fifty-three steps already," said Arnold.

"We're nearing the bottom," said Thomas.

The steps ended before a small door. Its surface was exquisitely decorated with typical examples of ancient Egyptian artistry. Over the door was a tablet inscribed with hieroglyphics.

"What does it say, Thomas?" asked Jerome. "You're the hieroglyphics expert."

"It says," said Thomas, squinting at the dim figures in the flickering lantern light, "'Beyond this door lies exalted Ikah-Mu-Kahma, fifth pharaoh of all Egypt. Let this be a warning to all who trespass. Death will come to those who enter his tomb. Ikah-Mu-Kahma will rise to avenge the disturbance of its sanctity.'"

Jerome Grabel's laughter was thin and tinged with nervousness. It rippled through the silence and echoed up the stairs of the shaft.

"Heh, heh. Typical of the warnings placed at the entrances to other pharaohs' tombs."

"They were supposed to scare off wandering bands of thieves, who might have broken into the tombs and stolen the treasures buried with the pharaoh," said Arnold.

He tried to push the door open, throwing all his weight against it.

"It's sealed," he panted at last.

"We'll have to smash it," said Thomas. "Lend a hand here, Jerome. Step away, Arnold."

Flinging their full weight against the sealed tomb-entrance door, Doctor Jerome Grabel and Professor Thomas Steel finally managed to break it down. What they saw on the other side sent them reeling.

"Look! On the floor!" gasped Arnold.

"Skeletons!" cried Jerome.

And skeletons there were indeed, piles and piles of them. The whitened skulls grinned up at them as if they each enjoyed a secret they would not share.

"Perhaps these are the remains of thieves who once broke in," ventured Jerome Grabel.

"Impossible. The door was sealed," said Arnold.

"Then who *are* they?"

"Workmen, perhaps. Servants who interred Ikah-Mu-Kahma and then were murdered so that the secret of the tomb's location would be kept."

Suddenly, Thomas Steel darted forward. "Jewels! Jewels!" he was shouting. "Arnold! Jerome! Come see!"

The other two turned to look into the corner where Thomas was yelling excitedly. "Good lord!" said Arnold. "It's a fortune in precious stones!"

Professor Thomas Steel scooped up handfuls of the sparkling gems. "Rubies! Emeralds! Sapphires! Millions of dollars' worth!"

"And the urns that hold them are solid gold!" added Jerome.

"This is the greatest archaeological discovery of the twentieth century!" declared Doctor Arnold Munsen. "I said it would be!"

"Take it easy, Arnold," cautioned Jerome. "Don't excite yourself. Remember—your heart."

Thomas Steel's voice came from a doorway a few feet away. "Here! In here!" he said, waving them over. "It's the burial chamber!"

The walls of the innermost sanctum were covered with ancient hieroglyphics. At its center was a stone coffin.

"The sarcophagus of Ikah-Mu-Kahma!" said Arnold in awe.

"Thomas! Help me lift the lid!" cried Jerome.

The two of them grabbed the ends, and with a mighty heave, the lid of the sarcophagus was off.

The three of them gasped when they saw the cloth-wrapped body inside.

"Perfectly preserved," said Thomas.

"What a find!" said Arnold. "We must get a message back to the museum at once!"

Thomas Steel just stared at Arnold Munsen. "But . . . but if we report that we've found the tomb . . . we'll have to turn the treasure over to them!" he said.

"Why—of course, Thomas!" said Arnold. "It belongs to them."

"But we found it!" protested Thomas. "We sweated and burned out in that hot sun until we discovered it! Isn't that right, Jerome?" Thomas turned to him in appeal.

But Jerome Grabel's face was hard with disapproval. "Thomas!" he rebuked his colleague. "I'm ashamed of you. Of course the treasure belongs to the museum."

But a minute later, while Arnold Munsen was examining the mummy, Jerome took Thomas by the arm and jerked him into a corner. "Shut up, you fool!" he hissed at Thomas. "Can't you see Arnold's too righteous to claim the treasure for himself?"

"Then we've got to get rid of him!" said Thomas. "He stands in our way."

Later that night, a hurried, whispered conversation took place in the camp of the three archaeologists.

"Is he asleep?" asked Thomas.

"Yes," answered Jerome. "Now this is what you do. Go down into the tomb. Unwrap the mummy of Ikah-Mu-Kahma, and wrap yourself in its windings. Then shout or scream. I'll awaken Arnold and tell him that you must be down there. When we reach the burial chamber, you go into a mummy act, and I'll start shouting about the curse."

"I get it," said Thomas, grinning. "His heart! He'll drop dead of fright."

"Exactly. And when we bring his body back to Cairo, we'll claim he had a heart attack from disappointment over the failure of our expedition."

"And the treasure will be ours," chuckled Thomas.

"All right," whispered Jerome. "Go ahead. And hurry!"

"Wait for my shout," said Thomas as he closed the flap of the tent.

Thomas Steel went down to the tomb. Jerome sat on his cot for a long time, growing more and more uneasy. Finally, he heard what he'd been waiting for:

"*Yaaaaaaaaaa!*"

Arnold woke and sat bolt upright on his cot, while Jerome Grabel leaped to his feet. Thomas's bloodcurdling scream came again.

"It's Thomas!" cried Arnold. "His bed's empty! He must be down there—in the tomb!"

"Let's go!" said Jerome, pulling on his pants. He was trying hard to look as worried as possible.

Arnold started down the tomb steps. Jerome followed. "He must be in trouble!" said Arnold.

"Hurry!" urged Jerome.

In a moment, they reached the treasure

chamber. Thomas's lamp sat upon the floor, illuminating the entire room. Beyond was the burial chamber. Arnold stopped.

"Oh, my lord, look!" he gasped.

"It's . . . it's the mummy!" cried Jerome. He was having real trouble keeping a straight face now.

It came from the burial chamber—tottering weakly, its windings hanging loosely. Jerome tried to keep his shoulders from shaking. Thomas looked so comical!

With some difficulty, Jerome went into his act. "The curse, Arnold!" he said in a quaking voice. "The curse on the entrance door!"

"'Death will come to those who enter his tomb. Ikah-Mu-Kahma . . . will . . . rise . . .'" quoted Arnold, choking on the words. His eyes were wide with terror.

The wrapped figure stumbled forward. "The curse is true, Arnold!" said Jerome. "The mummy has risen!"

"Jerome . . . I . . . I . . ." choked Arnold. But he couldn't get anything else out.

The mummy was almost upon them. "Arnold! Come on! Let's run!" yelled Jerome. "Run!"

Arnold Munsen's knees were collapsing. "Jerome . . ." he tried to say, gagging and wheezing. "My . . . my . . . heart!"

Clutching his chest, Arnold crumpled to the floor.

Jerome knelt down to examine him. He looked at the fixed pupils in the eyes, felt the chest for a heartbeat. "He's dead!" he said to himself when he was done.

Jerome stood up and began to laugh. The wrapped figure stopped.

"Good work, Thomas!" laughed Jerome. "Good work! Just one thing—"

Jerome drew the pistol he had hidden under his shirt.

"One thing you didn't count on, Thomas. You see, I want that treasure for myself. Thanks for your help." He laughed a sardonic laugh and fired at the mummy.

The bullet tore through its wrappings, but the mummy did not fall.

"For God's sake, I shot you, Thomas!" cried Jerome in a quivering voice. "I shot you! Die! *Die!*"

Jerome backed off, firing his gun again and again. But the mummy kept coming. Jerome

backed into the burial chamber.

The sarcophagus was open. Jerome stumbled backwards into it and spun to see what he had hit. "Good lord!" he gasped.

The man in the mummy case had a look of sheer horror on his face.

"Thomas! Thomas!" screamed Jerome, shaking the terror-stamped figure in the sarcophagus. But Thomas Steel was extremely dead.

"Then . . . then . . ." choked Jerome Grabel as the full realization hit him. The mummy was almost upon him. . . .

Hee, hee! So Ikah-Mu-what's-his-name took care of the disturbers of his sanctity, just as the curse had predicted. After that he tossed the bodies onto the pile with the other skeletons . . . yawned . . . shut the front slab once more . . . and went back to sleep. Which is more than you'll be able to do now that you've finished this little tale, isn't it? Well, maybe as long as you're up, you'd like to read the next one? It's very *soothing. Heh, heh.*

Listen up, my little pretties, because you're about to find out what used to go on in medical school. Let's hope it doesn't anymore. But just to be on the safe side, why don't you ask your doctor if she's in the Medical Corpse.

BARGAIN IN DEATH

My story has its beginning on a cool October evening in 1928. In their room in the dormitory of Loganwood Medical College, two young students sit dejectedly, their faces sullen.

"What can we do, Mel?" asks the one in the glasses. "Unless we raise some money, we won't be able to pay our laboratory fees."

"And without that lab course," says the other, straightening his green and white letter sweater, "we can't continue with our studies. Dissecting those cadavers is required for anatomy credit!"

"Cripes," complains Sid, the first student. "I didn't know stiffs cost so much. That's what the lab fee covers, you know."

"Yeah, I know," says Mel. He plays dispiritedly with his Loganwood key chain.

Suddenly, he gets an idea. "Say!" he cries. "What if we supplied our own corpse?"

"Huh?" says Sid. "How? You mean—"

"Don't look so shocked, Sid. It's been done before. We just dig up a fresh one in the town cemetery."

"*Steal a body?*" says Sid. "*Rob a grave?*"

"Either that, or we don't become doctors, Sid. Take your choice."

Meanwhile, far across town, the second scene of our grisly little yarn is taking place. There are two men in this scene, also. They look just a bit seedier than Sid and Mel, a bit older, a bit more down-at-the-heels. Life has dealt them a few knocks.

"It's crazy, Alex!" one of them is saying. He looks as if he hasn't seen sunlight in twenty years. "Absolutely crazy! I won't agree to it!"

"But it'll work, George!" says the other, the sharp-looking one with the slicked-back hair. "I know it will! I've seen what this drug can do! Besides, we need the money, don't we?"

"Yes, of course!" replies George. "But . . . to give up everything . . . start over . . ." He shakes his head.

"With twenty thousand dollars of insurance money," Alex reminds him.

George bows his head. "It *is* a lot of money," he says. "An awful lot."

"All you have to do," Alex explains, "is shoot this stuff into your arm. It cuts down your pulse and heartbeat—your entire metabolism—to such a point that the best doctor can't tell whether you are really dead or not. And don't worry about air. There'll be enough in the casket for the time you'll be in it.

"Then, after they bury you," he continues, grinning, "I'll come and dig you up. Since I'm the beneficiary of your life insurance policy, they'll have to pay me the forty thousand you're insured for! Then we'll split it."

"I . . . I don't know," says George. "It sounds good. But I'm afraid! Suppose . . . suppose there's a hitch?"

"Don't be a fool, George. What can go wrong?"

"Suppose the insurance company suspects?" says George.

"How can they?" counters Alex. "It'll look like heart failure. I'll be at home with a perfect alibi! No one else has any motive."

"How long will the effect of the drug last?" asks George.

"Thirty-six hours. You'll be unconscious. I'll make sure the funeral is rushed. There'll be no lying in state, no embalming. If you take it early in the morning, and they bury you the next day, I'll get you out that night. Thirty-six hours! Simple! Well, what do you say? For . . . twenty thousand dollars?"

As George paces the room, we go back to Scene One, where Sid and Mel the college boys are making their big decision. Everybody's got problems, it seems.

"All right, Mel," says Sid tremulously. "I'll do it."

"Atta boy, Sid!" says Mel, giving his room-mate a punch on the shoulder. "We'll get old Clem to help us. He'll do *anything* for money."

Back again (puff, puff, puff) to Scene Two, where the plot is sickening. George has now stopped pacing and is standing in the middle of the room, his head hanging, his hands jammed into his pockets. Of course, you know what he's going to say:

"I'll agree, Alex. But it's against my better judgment. . . ."

"Don't worry about it, George," says the confident Alex, smoothing back his Brylcreemed hair. "I'll take care of everything. Here's the hypodermic needle and the drug. Take a full shot.

"And for God's sake," he adds as he leaves the room, "get rid of the bottle and needle before the stuff takes effect! You'll have about ten minutes."

"I'll be careful, Alex," says George. "Don't worry."

So that's the situation, fiends. Like it? Good! Now for the complications! Ready? Here goes. The next morning, George's landlady discovers his body.

"*Eeeeeee!*" she shrieks predictably.

A doctor is summoned by the hysterical woman. He bends over George's pale body. "This man is dead," he pronounces. "Looks like heart failure. Must have happened early this morning."

He turns to the landlady. "Did he have any relatives?" he asks.

"No," she replies. "Only a friend. I'll go for him."

Alex receives the bad news convincingly. "*What?*" he cries. "George . . . dead? Good lord, what a shock! I'd better come back with you and make the arrangements."

"He . . . he was such a good man!" sobs the landlady. "Such a good man!"

And so, Alex arranges George's funeral. The undertaker is confused. "But it's customary to wait several days—" he protests.

"No!" says Alex. "George wouldn't have wanted it that way. The funeral will be held to-morrow—in the afternoon."

That evening, in their dormitory room, Sid and Mel are perusing the newspapers.

"Look, Sid!" exclaims Mel. "We're in luck! Some poor guy across town just died. They're burying him tomorrow afternoon!"

"Come," urges Sid. "Let's go see Clem. We'll dig up the body tomorrow night."

Sid and Mel find Clem, the college handyman, and explain their plan.

"Wal," he says slowly, scratching his head, "I dunno, fellers. Diggin' up a corpse! That's kinda scary business."

"We'll make it worth your while, Clem," says Mel. "Say . . . *five dollars?*"

"Wal . . . fer five dollars—I might."

"Good!" snaps Mel. "Meet us here tomorrow night!"

"Bring the tools!" adds Sid.

The next day, toward late afternoon, George—under the influence of the drug—is "laid to rest." Only Alex and the landlady are there to see it.

"He was a good man," sobs the landlady.

"Lower the coffin," says Alex.

After George's casket is lowered into the yawning black pit, the gravediggers step forward.

"C'mon, Zeke," says one. "Let's get it over

with. It's gettin' dark."

"Sure thing, Hank," says the other. They get to work.

From a distance, Alex, George's best friend and beneficiary, smiles as the soft earth is shoveled into George's grave. "Heh, heh," he chuckles to himself. "Won't you be surprised, George, when the drug wears off tonight . . . and I don't show up!"

A little while later, when Alex returns to his rooming house, a stranger is waiting for him.

"My name is Fogerty," says the man, tipping his hat. "I'm from Cosmopolitan Life. Are you Alex Lawrence?"

"That's me," smirks Alex.

"You are the beneficiary named in the forty-thousand dollar policy of the recently deceased George Arkman. . . ." begins the insurance man.

"Yes," says Alex. "Why? Anything wrong?" He's starting to sweat a little.

"No," says the man. "We've examined the certificate of death. Everything seems to be in order."

"Well, what do you want to see me about, then?"

The man pulls out a piece of paper. "Why, to present you with your check, Mister Lawrence. Here you are!"

"Oh! I . . . I . . . thank you!" Alex grabs for the check.

As darkness blankets the town and the little drab-looking cemetery, Alex Lawrence hastily packs. "Forty thousand dollars!" he chortles, throwing his few belongings into his suitcase. "Forty thousand! I'm rich!"

Meanwhile, deep down under the moldy black earth in the cemetery, something stirs. George is coming to.

"Huh?" he grunts. "Where . . . where am I? I . . . Oh! Now I remember. Oh, my God! I'm in a coffin—buried alive!"

George reaches up to the satin-lined lid of his underground prison and pushes hard. "I . . . can't . . . budge it! Oh, lord! How long can I last in here? Where's Alex? Why doesn't he come?"

At that moment, Alex stands in a used-car lot, surveying a shiny blue convertible.

"I'll take it," he tells the salesman. "Can I drive it off the lot?"

"Just as soon as we fill out the necessary papers, sir," the salesman replies. "Will you step into the office?"

Later that night, George still lies buried six feet below the cemetery's gravestone-bedecked surface. He is not doing so well. "Air . . . giving . . . out," he gasps. "Can't . . . last . . . much . . . longer! Oh, God! *Where's Alex?*"

Slowly the gate of the deserted cemetery swings open, its rusted hinges screaming in protest. Three figures enter: Sid and Mel and Clem.

"C'mon," says Mel. "This way." He tiptoes in past the gate, moonlight casting shadows across his path.

"I . . . I don' like this nohow," says Clem.

"Shhh, Clem," says Sid. "Remember the five bucks."

Gingerly, they make their way across the grave mounds to the fresh one.

"Here it is!" whispers Mel.

"Okay, Clem," orders Sid. "Start digging."

"Uh-huh," says Clem.

Down below, George hears a muffled thud, as Clem's spade cuts into the dank soil.

"It . . . it must be . . . Alex!" he cries. "Hurry . . . Alex! Hurry! I'm . . . suffocating!"

Little by little, Clem's spade gouges out an ever deepening hole as the minutes tick by.

"Just a little deeper, Clem!" Sid urges. "Just a little!"

"Uh-huh," says Clem, working at an infuriatingly slow pace.

"Hurry . . . Alex," George is still crying hoarsely. "Hurry . . . up!" He gasps for air.

At this moment, far across town, the motor of the blue convertible hums as Alex, at the wheel, guides it out of the lot.

"Good luck, sir," calls the salesman, waving good-bye to Alex. "Hope you like your new car."

"Yeah, thanks," says Alex, gunning the engine and screeching away from the curb.

Now the hollow boom of Clem's spade striking the coffin echoes across the deserted cemetery.

"Hurry! Pry open the lid!" says Sid.

"Here! Here's a crowbar," offers Mel.

"Uh-huh," says Clem.

Clem slips the sharp edge of the crowbar

81

under the lid and presses down. The coffin shudders, and then gives way.

"It's coming loose!" yells Mel.

"Lift it off, Clem!" says Sid.

"Uh-huh," says Clem.

George, gasping for air, drenched in perspiration, sits bolt upright in the coffin. Clem's eyes widen. He screams:

"*Yaaaaaaaah!*"

"Good lord!" hollers Mel.

Here comes Alex in his nice new shiny blue convertible. He's hitting eighty as he leaves town on the road that skirts the cemetery.

"Heh, heh!" he guffaws. "Hope you're comfortable in there, George."

Suddenly, two figures loom up before him in his headlights, scampering across the road. "Look out!" yells Alex—but of course, they can't hear him.

Alex swerves to avoid hitting the frightened students, who are running from the horrible sight in the cemetery. Alex's car hurtles across the road toward the cemetery fence, crashes into it, and flips over among the tombstones.

Alex's last word is "*Eeeaaaaaagh!*"

Later, in a dark corner of a local bar, Sid

and Mel compose themselves with several shots of hard liquor.

"Lord, Mel!" pants Sid. "If I didn't see it with my own eyes, I wouldn't have believed it! That corpse actually sat up!"

"And that poor guy in the convertible!" said Mel. "He tried to avoid hitting *us* and killed *himself!*"

Finally, Sid and Mel return to their room.

"The less said about tonight, the better," Mel advises as Sid puts his key into the lock.

"Gee, I wonder what happened to Clem?" says Sid.

"Here I is!" calls Clem, who is waiting inside the room. "I been waitin' on yuh."

"Clem!" Sid exclaims.

"That'll be five bucks, please," says Clem in his slow, deliberate way. "That's what yuh promised me fer the body."

"Good lord, Sid! Look!"

Mel points across the room with a shaking finger.

The two medical students stare in horror at the prostrate body stretched out on the floor. It is George Arkman, his head crushed by the blow of Clem's crowbar. . . .

Heh, heh! Yep, old Clem really came across—by George! Sid and Mel got the stiff they needed. Now they both have very successful medical practices and BMW's. As for poor Alex . . . he came in handy for that week's Anatomy 101 class at good old Loganwood Medical College.

 *And now, my little pumpernickels, we've reached the end of the road for this weighty tome. I've decided that it's only fair for you, like Ernie, to have the—*

LAST LAUGH

Ernie shifted uncomfortably on the chair in the doctor's waiting room. From time to time the expression on his loose, flabby-featured face would change from a worried frown to a cheerful grin, and he would chuckle silently or laugh out loud. When that happened, he would clutch his stomach, and the grin would fade and the anxiety would return once more. He shook his head sadly after his most recent outburst of hilarity and looked up with relief as Dr. Falder entered the waiting room.

"I'm sorry I kept you waiting, sir," said the doctor, slipping out of his overcoat, "but I've been having personal difficulties at home. Your call seemed urgent. What's the trouble?"

"It's my stomach, Doc," said Ernie. "I got pains. It hurts me every time I laugh."

"All right," said the doctor with a sigh. "We'll take a look at you. If you'll step this way, Mr.—Mr.—I'm afraid I didn't catch the name. . . ."

"Ceely, Doc. Ernie Ceely. I'm new 'round these parts. Been in town about two weeks."

The doctor led Ernie into his examination room and rolled up his sleeves.

"Might as well give you a thorough going-over, Mr. Ceely. While I'm examining you, you can tell me about this pain you've been having."

"Started last week," said Ernie. "I musta strained myself or something."

The doctor bent over the sink and began to wash his hands. "Strained yourself, Mr. Ceely?" he inquired. "How? Oh . . . if you'll please remove your shirt . . ."

"Sure, Doc. Yeah, that's what I figure happened. Yuh see, Doc, I go for yaks."

Doctor Falder looked at Ernie quizzically as he dried his hands. "Go for yaks, Mr. Ceely? I don't understand."

"Yaks, doc. Laughs! Large charges! I get a

86

bang out of jokes—practical jokes. Stuff like I call up a number, any old number, some night, and I say, 'This is the electric company, madam. We're checking on the street lamps in your area. Would you kindly look and see if the street lamp outside your house is lit?' And the lady says—it's best if it's an old lady—'Of course, hold on please.' So the sucker goes, see. An' when they come back, they say, 'Yes, the street lamp outside my house is lit.' And then *I* say, 'Well, be sure to put it out before you go to bed, huh, honey? Bye!'"

Ernie Ceely began to laugh uproariously.

"They . . . heh . . . they fall for it every time, Doc . . . heh, heh. They . . . Ooooh! It hurts!"

The doctor slipped into his white lab coat. "I see" was all the doctor said.

"An' last week," Ernie said, "I nearly died laughin'. I pulled this gag, see. And I figure I musta strained myself laughin' over it."

Ernie stood before the doctor, stripped to the waist, the examining room lights reflecting on his obese body. Doc Falder placed his stethoscope to his ears.

"Breathe deeply and hold it," said the doc-

tor, pressing the stethoscope to Ernie's chest. He was not smiling.

The doctor moved the stethoscope about Ernie's chest, listening grimly. "All right," he said. "Exhale. Go on, Mr. Ceely."

"Or I call up a candy store," said Ernie, giggling, "an' I say, 'Rosie's Candy Store? Do you have Butterfingers?' and she goes and checks and comes back and says, 'Yes, sir.' And then I say, 'Well, don't drop anything!'"

The doctor folded away his stethoscope as Ernie guffawed heartily again.

"Stuff like that. Heh, heh! What a riot! Heh, heh! I . . . Oooooh!" He grimaced.

"And last week?" said the doctor. "You say last week you seemed to strain yourself?"

Doctor Falder wrapped the blood-pressure bag around Ernie's arm. Ernie nodded, grinning.

"Doc! Last week I pulled the greatest . . . the craziest . . . the best yak I ever pulled! I tell you, I nearly died laughin'."

"And what was that, Mr. Ceely?" asked the doctor.

Ernie started to chuckle. "I get this idea, see? I notice that the kids in this town all play down by the railroad tracks. An' I notice that the train shoots through, doin' about seventy, every day at noon.

"So last week, I buy me some hunks of horse meat. Real cheap stuff. Big an' raw an' bloody. An' I buy me some kids' clothes. An' I stuff the meat in the kids' clothes, and I go down to the tracks about noon, and I lay the mess on the tracks near where some kids is playin'. And I wait, an' when the train shoots by, I scream.

" 'Hey! What was that?' one of the kids says. 'Somebody screamed!'

"Doc, you should have seen the faces on those kids! They took one look at the gory mess, and they started runnin' in all directions!"

Ernie clutched at his stomach, wincing and giggling alternately. "Honest, Doc. I nearly croaked. You should have seen their faces. Soon, the whole town come out. It took 'em maybe three hours before they found out it weren't no kid got killed. Sirens, and ambulances, runnin' around like crazy!" He slapped his knee.

The doctor just shook his head. "And meanwhile you're . . . laughing," he said.

"Dyin'!" Ernie agreed mirthfully.

"Wait here, Mr. Ceely. I'll be back in a moment." Doc Falder left Ernie alone in the examination room. After a few moments, he came back with four capsules in one hand and a glass of water in the other.

"Here, Mr. Ceely," he said. "Swallow these."

"D'yuh know what's wrong, Doc?" asked Ernie. "Will I be all right?" He took the capsules and swallowed them.

"You'll be fine, Mr. Ceely. And now I want

you to go out into the waiting room and sit down. I'll call you when I'm ready. I want to perform some tests on you."

"Sure, Doc. Sure," said Ernie.

Ernie went out into the waiting room and sat down. He could hear Dr. Falder moving equipment around behind the closed examination room door.

"Just relax, Mr. Ceely," called the doctor. "I'll be ready for you shortly."

"Okay, Doc."

Fifteen minutes went by, and Ernie began to grow impatient. Twenty minutes. Ernie felt a funny, sharp pain in his stomach. Finally, the doctor came out.

"I'm ready, Mr. Ceely. Will you come in now?"

"Doc!" said Ernie. "Somethin's happenin'! Here, in my stomach! It hurts, even when I don't laugh."

Ernie followed the doctor into the examination room once more.

"Get completely undressed, Mr. Ceely," directed the doctor, "except for your shorts. And while you're doing that, listen to what I have to say."

"Okay, Doc," said Ernie. "But see what you can do about these new pains I got now, huh?"

The doctor nodded grimly, watching Ernie disrobe. He began to talk.

"There was a family in this town, Mr. Ceely," he said. "A mother, a father, and two children—boys—one, eight; the young one, three . . ."

"Can't stand kids," said Ernie. "Boy, you should have seen their faces when they saw that bloody mess."

"One day," the doctor continued, "the mother sent her two boys out to play. She told the eight-year-old to watch the three-year-old and keep him out of mischief. 'See that Stevey doesn't get himself dirty, Jeffrey,' she said to him.

"But the eight-year-old wandered away, and he left the three-year-old. And the three-year-old got all muddy playing where he shouldn't have. He came home alone, a mess, and his mother was annoyed.

"The eight-year-old had gone to play with his friends by the railroad tracks. He'd completely forgotten about his little three-year-old brother until he heard a bloodcurdling scream

as the train hurtled by. 'Stevey!' he cried.

"Jeffrey thought that the bloody remains lying on the railroad tracks were his younger brother, Stevey. Fear clutched at his little eight-year-old heart. He started running home wildly.

"He never saw the truck bearing down upon him in the street.

"The mother rushed out of her house when she heard her older son's shriek of pain and the squeal of the truck's brakes. 'Jeffrey! My baby!' she shrieked.

"In her frightened anxiety, the mother had thoughtlessly left her three-year-old son crying, in the tub where she'd been bathing him."

Ernie stood before the doctor, staring at his wide, flaming eyes.

"You!" he gasped.

"Yes, Mr. Ceely," said the doctor. "That was my family's story. The eight-year-old boy died from being struck by the truck. The baby drowned. My wife dropped dead of a heart attack."

Dr. Falder's grip was like a vise of steel as he tied Ernie Ceely to the examination table. "You say you almost died laughing over your little practical joke, Mr. Ceely? Well, now you *will* die laughing! Those capsules I gave you contained poison. The poison will make your stomach bleed. The more you laugh, the more your stomach will bleed. It will take you a few hours to die."

"No! No!" squealed Ernie.

Dr. Falder rolled out the equipment he'd prepared and set it about the stripped, reclining figure of screaming Ernie Ceely. Then the doctor turned all of the equipment on. And the feathers tickled the soles of Ernie's feet and brushed his ribs and under his arms and behind his ears.

"Die laughing, Ernie!" said the doctor, standing over him. "*Die laughing!*"

Ernie began laughing. And he laughed, and he laughed, and he laughed. . . .

Well, I guess this is what they mean by <u>yucking it up,</u> huh? And pretty yucky it is, too. That Ernie, he was a real <u>scream</u> right up until the end. He certainly seemed <u>tickled to death</u> to find a good doctor. But aren't we all?

Well, it's time for me to climb onto the old broomstick, make like a tree, and get out of here. See you around the cauldron!